The Party in the Sky

For James, Clare and Paul

A Red Fox Book

Published by Random Century Children's Books
20 Vauxhall Bridge Road, London SW1V 2SA
A division of the Random Century Group

London Melbourne Sydney Auckland
Johannesburg and agencies throughout the world

First published in Great Britain by
Hutchinson Children's Books 1990

Red Fox edition 1992

© Alison Catley 1990

Printed in Singapore

Alison Catley

The Party in the Sky

RED FOX

My name is Claire and I live in Flat 54 on the tenth floor of Beechwood Towers. It was my birthday on Saturday. I was six and I had a party.

I made the invitations myself. There were eleven all together, with a special one for my best friend Paul. I drew a fire-breathing dragon on his envelope, because dragons and castles are my favourite things.

I handed out my invitations at school. Most people were really excited, but Christopher said, 'How can you have a proper party if you live in a flat? You haven't even got a garden to play in.' Then he sang, 'Poky little flat, poky little flat, not enough room to swing a cat.'

After school I talked to Paul about my party. He told me not to take any notice of Christopher; but I kept thinking, how *could* I have a proper party without a garden? If only I lived in a castle, with a drawbridge and a big green dragon guarding the gate . . . .

When I got home I read my dragon book and wouldn't talk to Mum. She asked me what the matter was.

'I hate living in a flat,' I said. 'How can I have a proper party without a garden to play in?'

'Not everyone can have a garden,' Mum whispered, pulling me on to her lap.

But I couldn't help sulking. 'I wish we lived in a castle,' I said.

The next day, strange things started happening. I found some big rolls of paper behind the curtain and there was sticky tape all over the floor. Mum and Dad were whispering all the time and they wouldn't tell me what they were saying. It was as if they had a big secret. As my party got closer the flat seemed to get more and more untidy. What was going on?

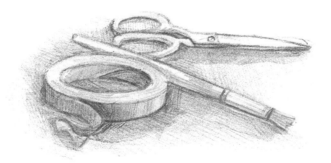

By the time Saturday arrived, I didn't feel like having a party at all. I even hoped I'd get a cold, or a temperature, or even the measles! But I didn't.

Everything seemed to be upside down, and there was a notice on the living room door. It said:

KEEP OUT UNTIL THE PARTY, OR ELSE!

I had to push my way into Mum and Dad's room. I couldn't believe it! It was full of our living room furniture! All that I could see of Dad were his toes sticking out from the end of the bed.

'Happy birthday,' he said.

It didn't feel like a happy birthday at all.

The first surprise was in the kitchen. I found a huge castle cake with a big green dragon on top. 'Where did that come from?' I said.

'Magic,' said Mum.

I had my breakfast and my bath, but I still wasn't allowed into the living room! I tried to peek through the keyhole, but even that was covered up. Something exciting was definitely going on.

Then, at last, it was three o'clock – time to put on my party dress and open the door . . . .

I couldn't believe it! A castle! Mum and Dad had made the room into a fantastic castle with stone walls and a big fire-breathing dragon painted on the windows.

I spun round and round and round. My birthday was going to be wonderful after all.

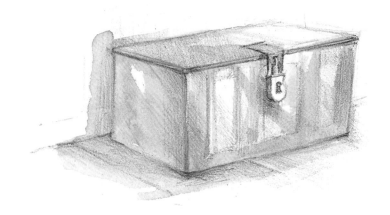

Paul was the first to arrive. 'Wow!' he said when he saw the room. 'It's a castle in the sky.'

We had jelly and crisps and special castle sandwiches. Best of all was my birthday cake, but I wouldn't let anyone eat the dragon on top. I wanted to save him for ever.

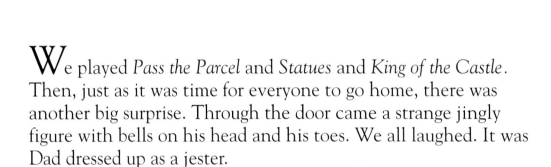

We played *Pass the Parcel* and *Statues* and *King of the Castle*.
Then, just as it was time for everyone to go home, there was
another big surprise. Through the door came a strange jingly
figure with bells on his head and his toes. We all laughed. It was
Dad dressed up as a jester.

There was a puff of pink smoke and out from the box came
balloons and streamers and hopping frogs. Everyone had a
special present to take home.

Suddenly my party was over. Mum put the presents into bags and I went to the door to say goodbye. Everyone said it was the best party ever, even Christopher. Paul was the last to go. I'm glad he's my best friend.

I was so happy I didn't want to go to bed. After all, the next day my castle would be gone for ever.

But Mum and Dad said, as a special treat, they would let me sleep in my castle room. As I snuggled under the covers I thought, who needs a garden when you've got a castle in the sky – and a Mum and Dad like mine!